# THE GREAT
# KAPOK TREE

# Tropical Rain Forests

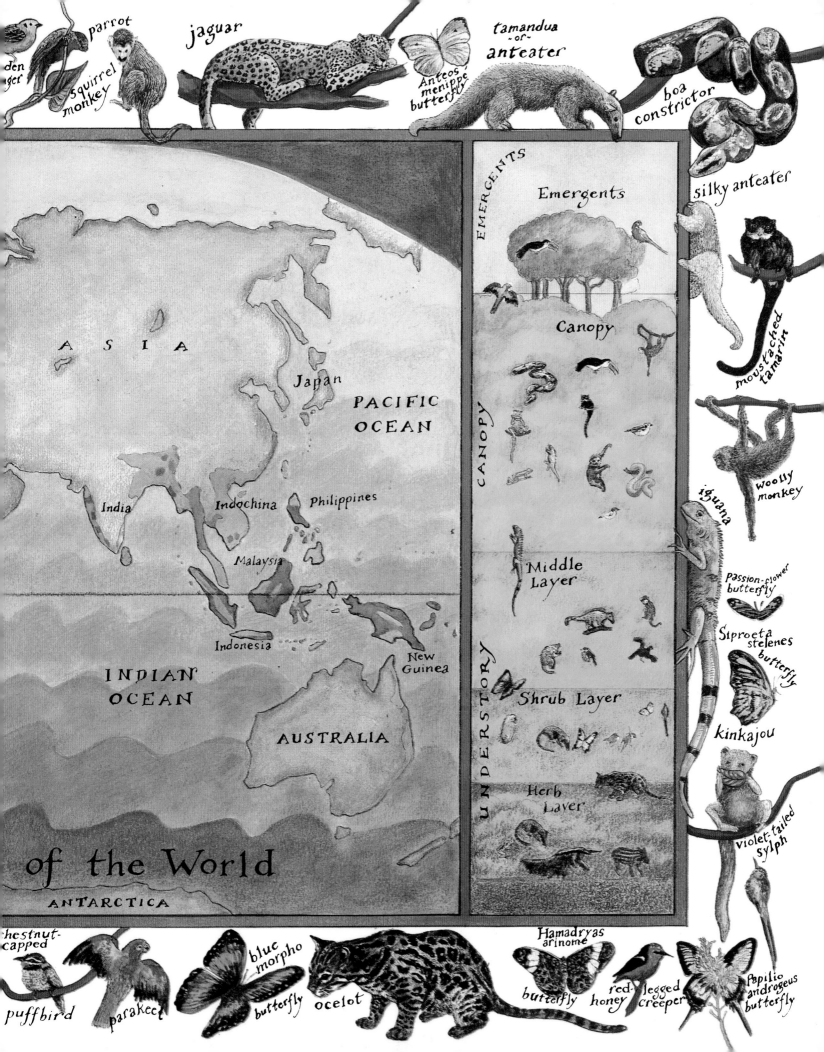

tiger

parrot

squirrel monkey

jaguar

Anteos menippe butterfly

tamandua ~or~ anteater

boa constrictor

silky anteater

moustached tamarin

woolly monkey

iguana

passion-flower butterfly

Siproeta stelenes butterfly

kinkajou

violet-tailed sylph

EMERGENTS

Emergents

Canopy

CANOPY

Middle Layer

UNDERSTORY

Shrub Layer

Herb Layer

ASIA

Japan

PACIFIC OCEAN

India

Indochina

Philippines

Malaysia

Indonesia

New Guinea

INDIAN OCEAN

AUSTRALIA

of the World

ANTARCTICA

chestnut-capped puffbird

parakeet

blue morpho butterfly

ocelot

Hamadryas arinome butterfly

red-legged honey creeper

Papilio androgeus butterfly

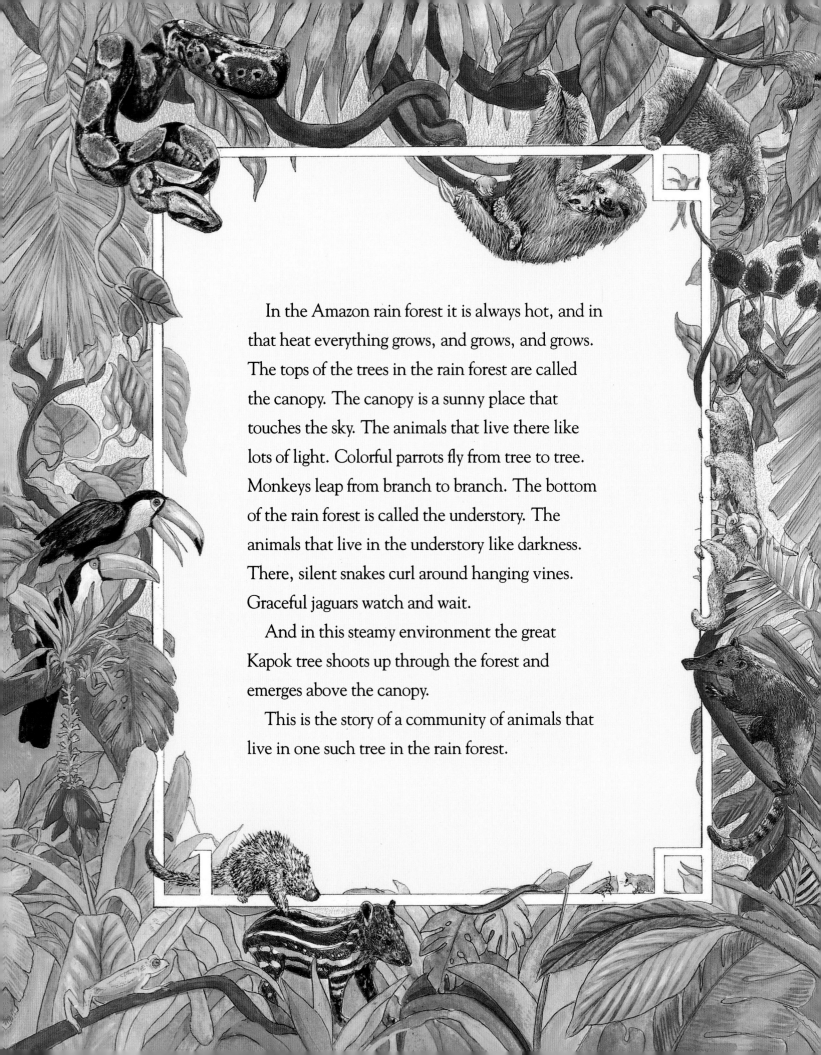

In the Amazon rain forest it is always hot, and in that heat everything grows, and grows, and grows. The tops of the trees in the rain forest are called the canopy. The canopy is a sunny place that touches the sky. The animals that live there like lots of light. Colorful parrots fly from tree to tree. Monkeys leap from branch to branch. The bottom of the rain forest is called the understory. The animals that live in the understory like darkness. There, silent snakes curl around hanging vines. Graceful jaguars watch and wait.

And in this steamy environment the great Kapok tree shoots up through the forest and emerges above the canopy.

This is the story of a community of animals that live in one such tree in the rain forest.

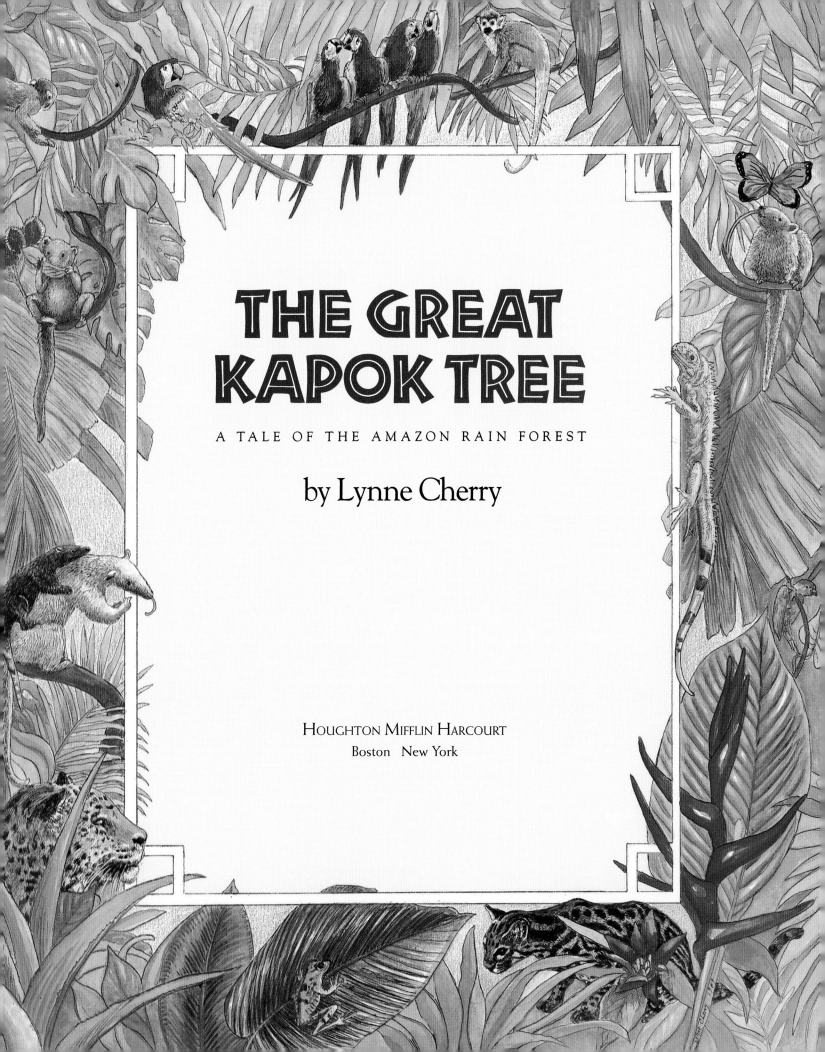

# THE GREAT KAPOK TREE

A TALE OF THE AMAZON RAIN FOREST

by Lynne Cherry

HOUGHTON MIFFLIN HARCOURT
Boston   New York

Thanks to my friends Irv and Bernice Kirk for their editorial assistance; to the World Wildlife
Fund in Washington, D.C., and especially to Rob Bierregaard for sharing his office, his reference
photos and his expertise; to Victor Bullen, and again, to Rob for facilitating my trip to WWF's
base camp in the Amazon rain forest and to Carlos Miller, the native Brazilian who posed as the
woodcutter, to Brian Boom, assistant curator at the New York Botanical Garden, for all his assistance, especially in Manaus; to Stephen Nash and Judy Stone of SUNY at Stonybrook; to Russ
Mittermeier, Marc Plotkin, and Gary Hartshorn of the World Wildlife Fund and Tom Lovejoy of
the Smithsonian Institution. A special thanks to Eric Fersht for his help every step of the way, and
as always, to my folks, Herbert and Helen Cherry.

Because this story is about the Amazon rain forest, the Brazilian spelling *senbor* has been used.

The illustrations in this book were done in watercolors, colored pencils, and Dr. Martin's
Watercolors on Strathmore 400 watercolor paper.

Library of Congress Cataloging-in-Publication Data
Cherry, Lynne.
The great kapok tree: a tale of the Amazon rain forest/by Lynne Cherry.
p.  cm.
Summary: The many different animals that live in a great kapok tree in the
Brazilian rain forest try to convince a man with an ax of the importance of not
cutting down their home.
[1. Conservation of natural resources — Fiction.   2. Rain forests—Fiction.
3. Ecology — Fiction.   4. Kapok — Fiction.]   I. Title.
PZ7.C4199Gr   1990
[E] — dc19      89-2208
ISBN 978-0-15-200520-7

ISBN 978-0-15-202614-1 pb
ISBN 978-0-15-201818-4 big book
ISBN 978-0-15-232320-2 Spanish pb

SCP   55 54 53 52 51 50 49 48
4500794145

Printed in China

*This book is dedicated to the memory of
Chico Mendes,
who gave his life in order to preserve
a part of the rain forest.*

Two men walked into the rain forest.
Moments before, the forest had been alive
with the sounds of squawking birds and
howling monkeys. Now all was quiet as
the creatures watched the two men and
wondered why they had come.

The larger man stopped and pointed to a
great Kapok tree. Then he left.

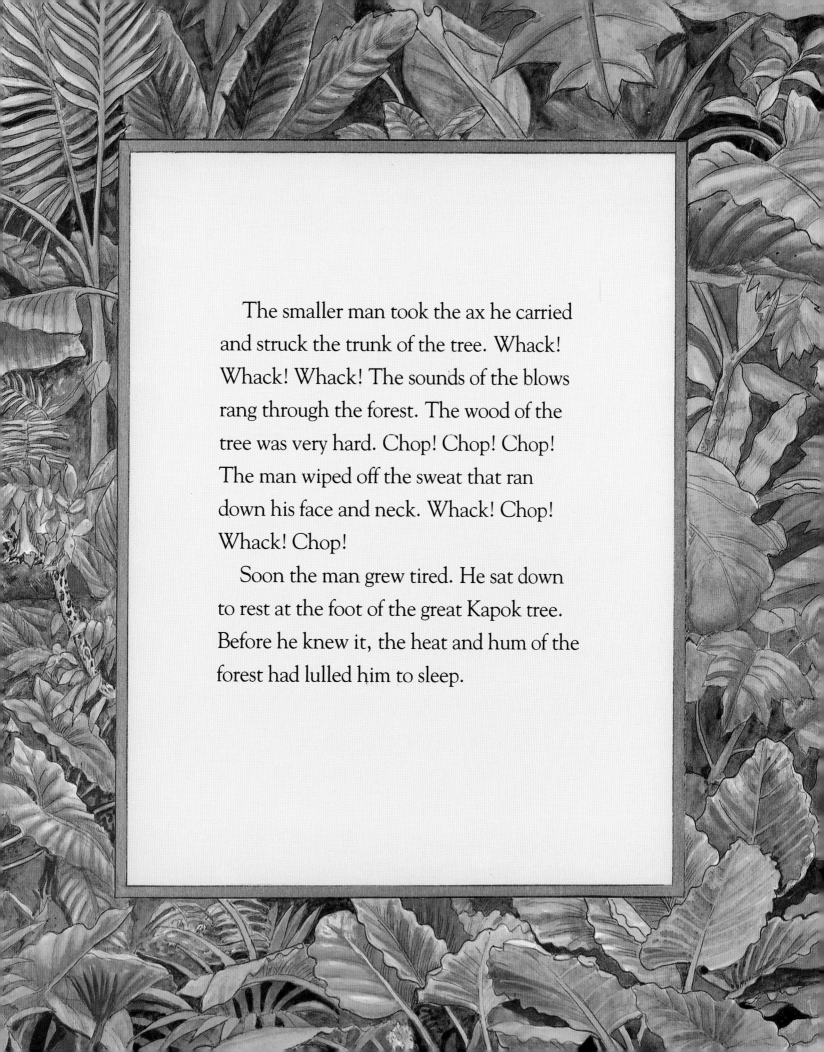

The smaller man took the ax he carried
and struck the trunk of the tree. Whack!
Whack! Whack! The sounds of the blows
rang through the forest. The wood of the
tree was very hard. Chop! Chop! Chop!
The man wiped off the sweat that ran
down his face and neck. Whack! Chop!
Whack! Chop!

Soon the man grew tired. He sat down
to rest at the foot of the great Kapok tree.
Before he knew it, the heat and hum of the
forest had lulled him to sleep.

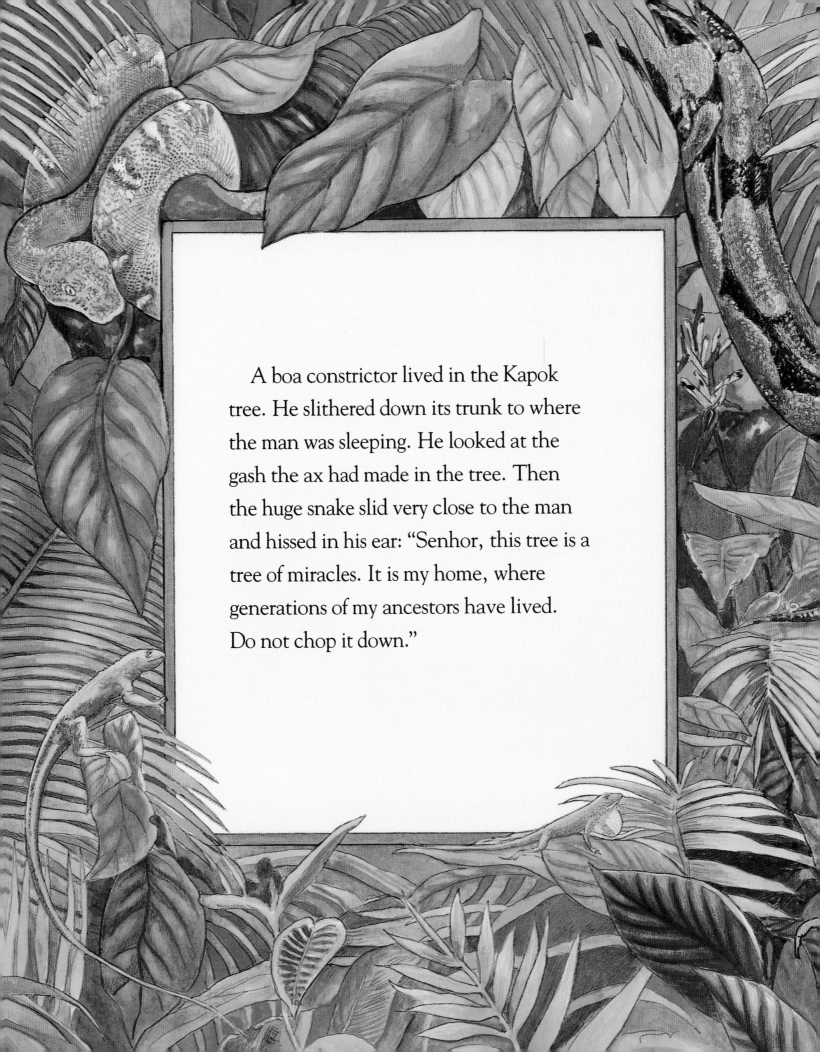

A boa constrictor lived in the Kapok tree. He slithered down its trunk to where the man was sleeping. He looked at the gash the ax had made in the tree. Then the huge snake slid very close to the man and hissed in his ear: "Senhor, this tree is a tree of miracles. It is my home, where generations of my ancestors have lived. Do not chop it down."

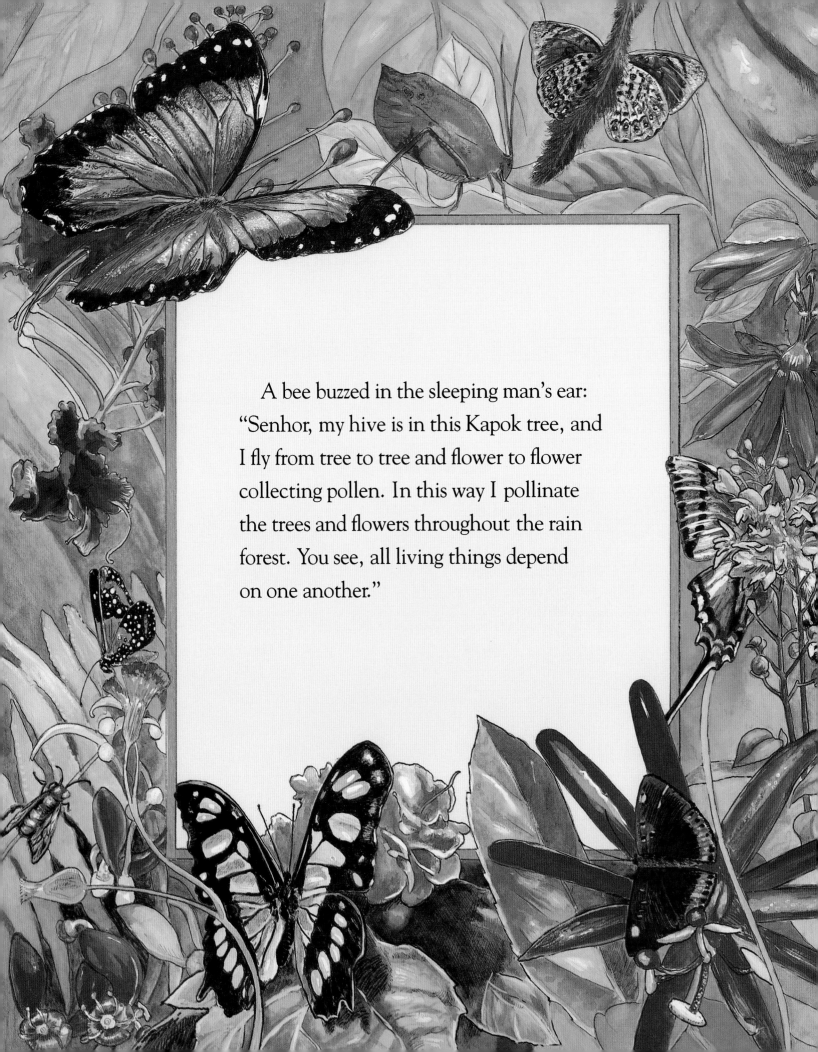

A bee buzzed in the sleeping man's ear:
"Senhor, my hive is in this Kapok tree, and
I fly from tree to tree and flower to flower
collecting pollen. In this way I pollinate
the trees and flowers throughout the rain
forest. You see, all living things depend
on one another."

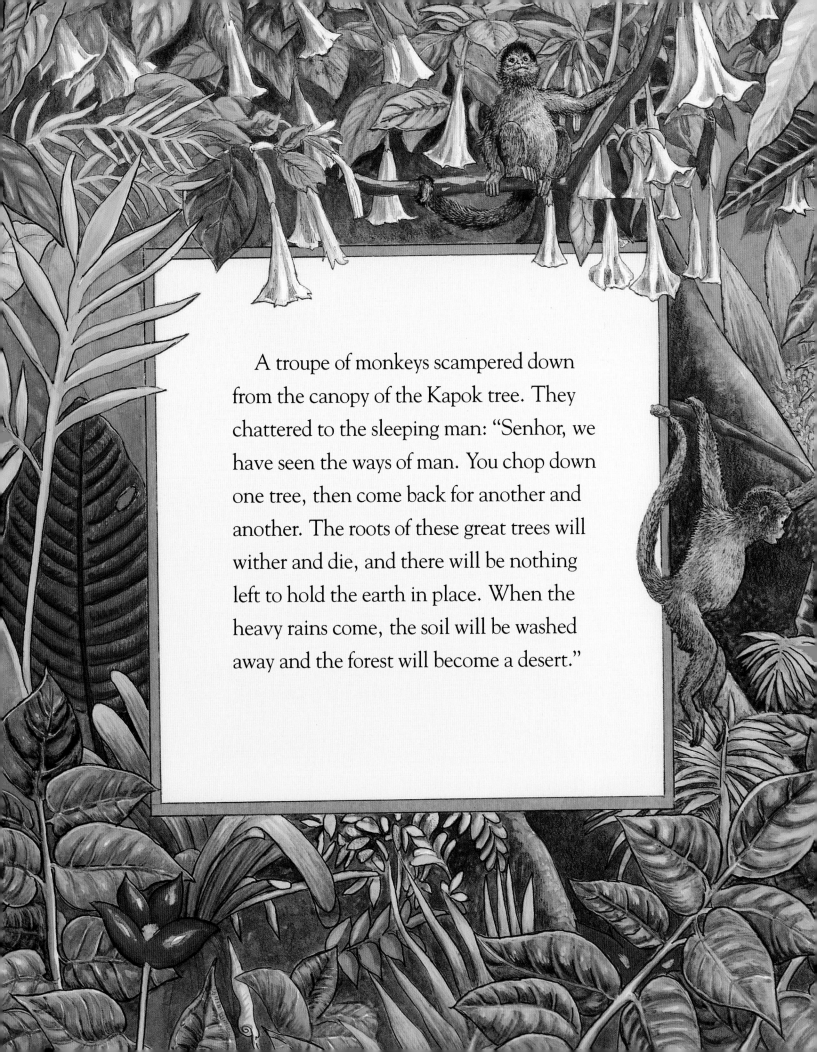

A troupe of monkeys scampered down from the canopy of the Kapok tree. They chattered to the sleeping man: "Senhor, we have seen the ways of man. You chop down one tree, then come back for another and another. The roots of these great trees will wither and die, and there will be nothing left to hold the earth in place. When the heavy rains come, the soil will be washed away and the forest will become a desert."

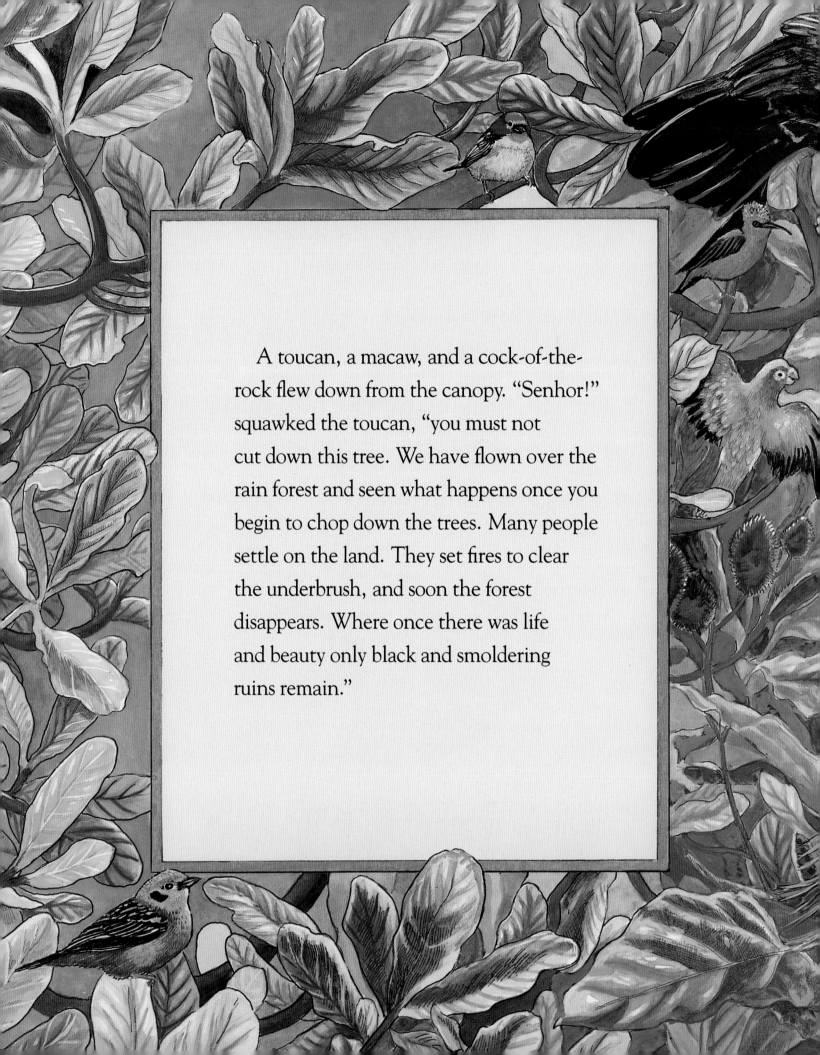

A toucan, a macaw, and a cock-of-the-rock flew down from the canopy. "Senhor!" squawked the toucan, "you must not cut down this tree. We have flown over the rain forest and seen what happens once you begin to chop down the trees. Many people settle on the land. They set fires to clear the underbrush, and soon the forest disappears. Where once there was life and beauty only black and smoldering ruins remain."

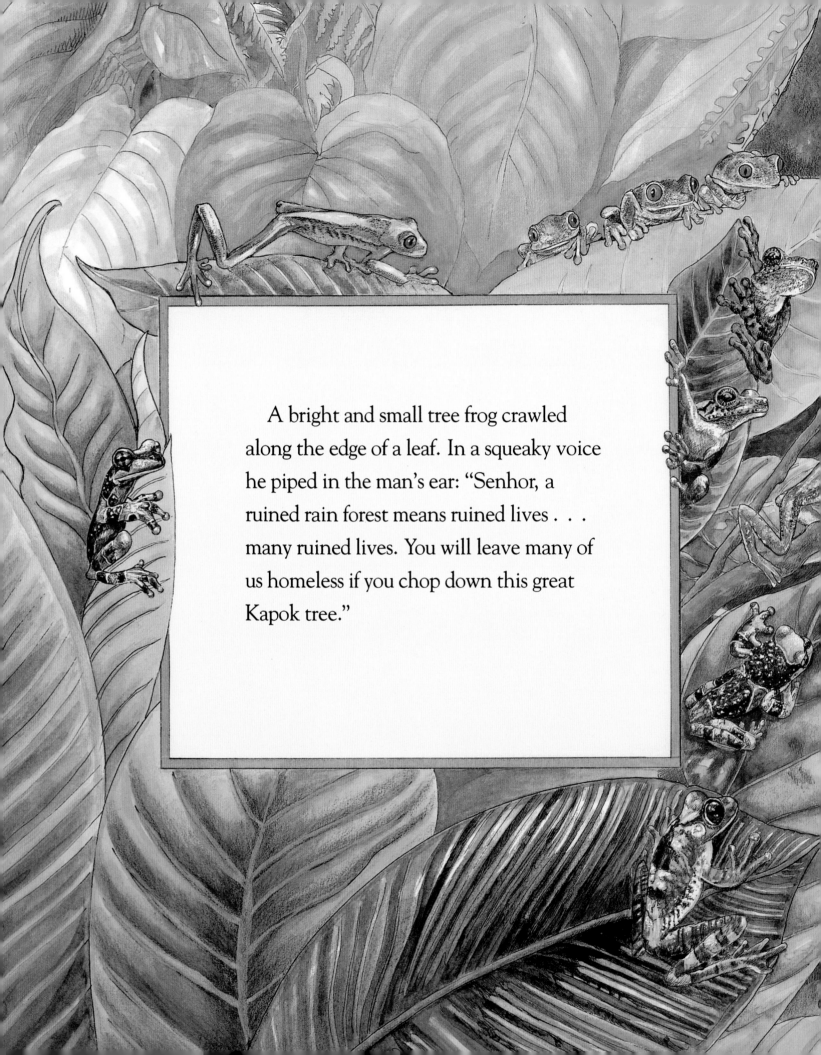

A bright and small tree frog crawled
along the edge of a leaf. In a squeaky voice
he piped in the man's ear: "Senhor, a
ruined rain forest means ruined lives . . .
many ruined lives. You will leave many of
us homeless if you chop down this great
Kapok tree."

A jaguar had been sleeping along a branch in the middle of the tree. Because his spotted coat blended into the dappled light and shadows of the understory, no one had noticed him. Now he leapt down and padded silently over to the sleeping man. He growled in his ear: "Senhor, the Kapok tree is home to many birds and animals. If you cut it down, where will I find my dinner?"

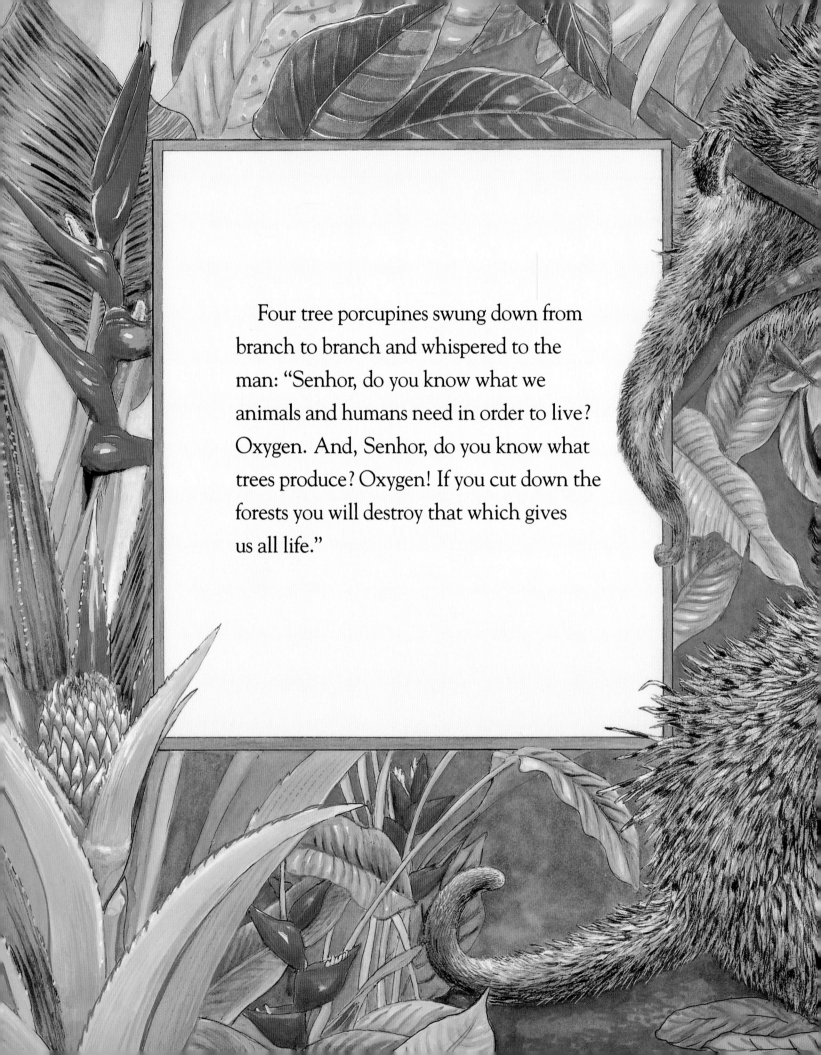

Four tree porcupines swung down from branch to branch and whispered to the man: "Senhor, do you know what we animals and humans need in order to live? Oxygen. And, Senhor, do you know what trees produce? Oxygen! If you cut down the forests you will destroy that which gives us all life."

Several anteaters climbed down the Kapok tree with their young clinging to their backs. The unstriped anteater said to the sleeping man: "Senhor, you are chopping down this tree with no thought for the future. And surely you know that what happens tomorrow depends upon what you do today. The big man tells you to chop down a beautiful tree. He does not think of his own children, who tomorrow must live in a world without trees."

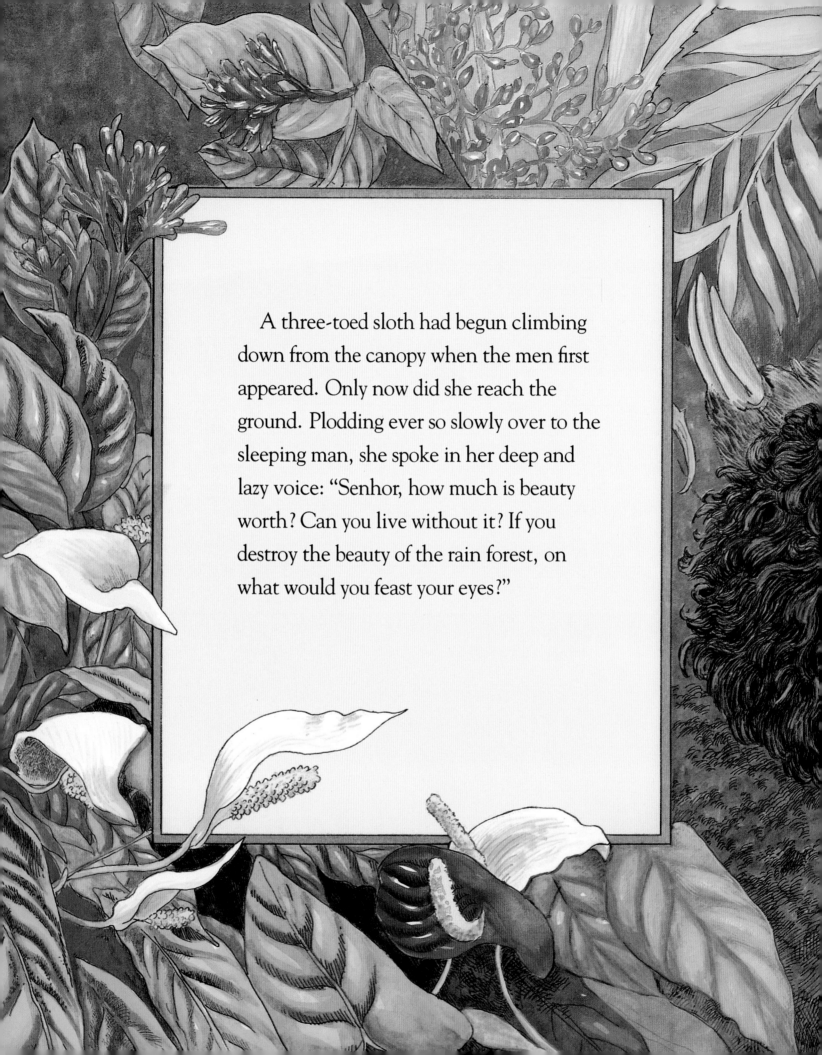

A three-toed sloth had begun climbing down from the canopy when the men first appeared. Only now did she reach the ground. Plodding ever so slowly over to the sleeping man, she spoke in her deep and lazy voice: "Senhor, how much is beauty worth? Can you live without it? If you destroy the beauty of the rain forest, on what would you feast your eyes?"

A child from the Yanomamo tribe who lived in the rain forest knelt over the sleeping man. He murmured in his ear: "Senhor, when you awake, please look upon us all with new eyes."

The man awoke with a start. Before him
stood the rain forest child, and all around
him, staring, were the creatures who
depended upon the great Kapok tree. What
wondrous and rare animals they were!

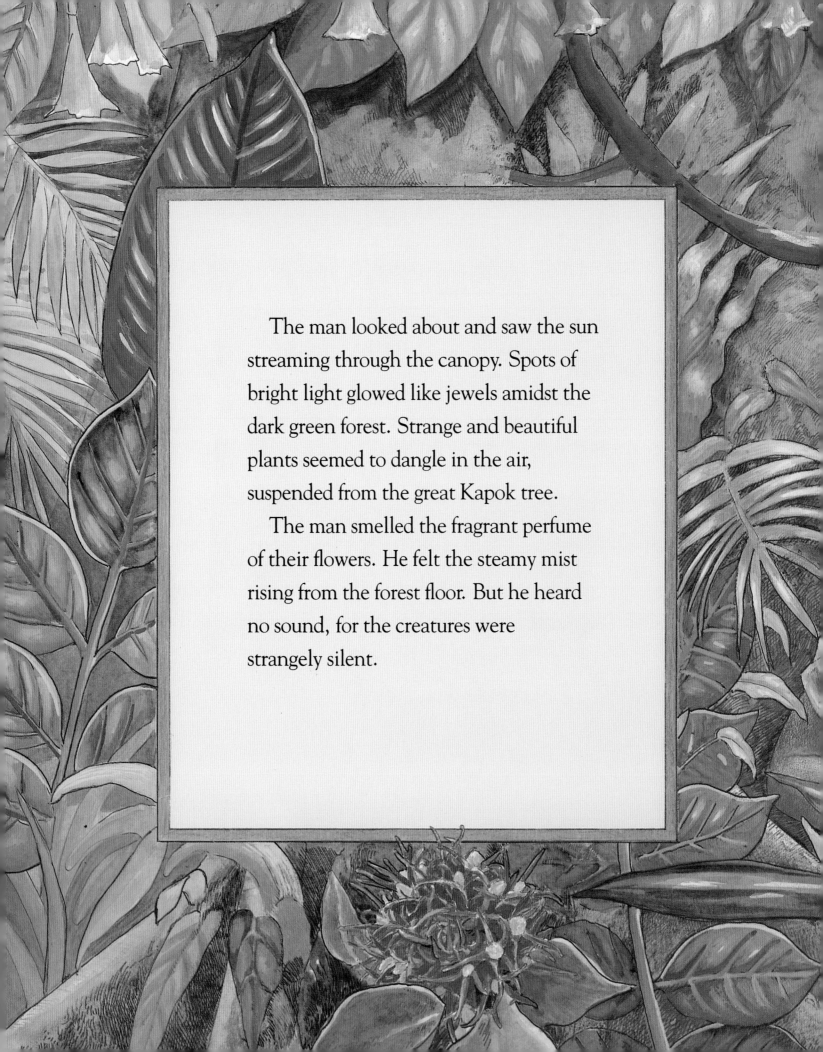

The man looked about and saw the sun streaming through the canopy. Spots of bright light glowed like jewels amidst the dark green forest. Strange and beautiful plants seemed to dangle in the air, suspended from the great Kapok tree.

The man smelled the fragrant perfume of their flowers. He felt the steamy mist rising from the forest floor. But he heard no sound, for the creatures were strangely silent.

The man stood and picked up his ax. He swung back his arm as though to strike the tree. Suddenly he stopped. He turned and looked at the animals and the child.

He hesitated. Then he dropped the ax
and walked out of the rain forest.

DEAR READERS,

I WROTE THE GREAT KAPOK TREE
TO LET THE WORLD KNOW WHAT
HAPPENS TO THE RAIN FOREST
CREATURES AND TO THE ENTIRE
PLANET WHEN RAIN FORESTS ARE
DESTROYED.

I HOPE THAT AFTER READING
THIS BOOK YOU WILL HELP SAVE
THE RAIN FORESTS. THE GREAT KAPOK TREE
IS ABOUT THE AMAZON RAIN FOREST —
A TROPICAL RAIN FOREST — BUT WE HAVE
A TEMPERATE RAIN FOREST IN THE
PACIFIC NORTHWEST OF THE UNITED
STATES THAT WE MUST PROTECT, TOO.

PLEASE CARE FOR MOTHER EARTH. TOGETHER
WE CAN MAKE A DIFFERENCE !

Lynne Cherry

emerald
tree boa

scarlet
macaw

Brazilian
tree frog

coati

scamander

toucan

red-necked
tanager

tree
frog

three-toed sloth

ARCTIC OCEAN

GREENLAND

EUROPE

NORTH
AMERICA

AFRICA

urania
butterfly

Central
America

CARIBBEAN
SEA

ATLANTIC
OCEAN

Equator

cock-of-the-rock

THE
AMAZON RAIN FOREST

Rio Negro

Manaus

AMAZON RIVER

Brazil

SOUTH
AMERICA

Madagascar

tree
porcupine

PACIFIC
OCEAN

today's rain forests

original extent of rain forests

Tropical Rain Forests

mother &
baby tapir

mother & baby
giant anteater

Vindula
arsinoë
butterfly

baby
hoatzin

Amazonian
katydid

poison
arrow
frog

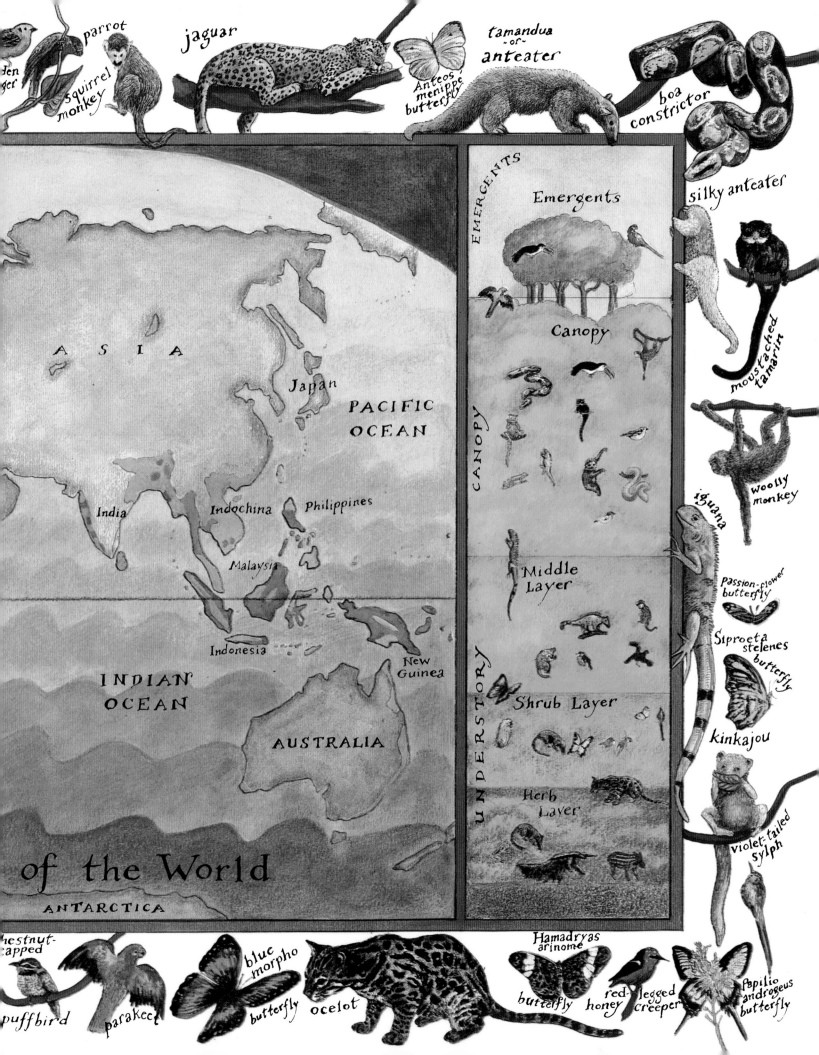

parrot

jaguar

tamandua
~or~
anteater

squirrel
monkey

Anteos
menippe
butterfly

boa
constrictor

silky anteater

Emergents

moustached
tamarin

Canopy

A S I A

Japan

PACIFIC
OCEAN

woolly
monkey

iguana

India

Indochina

Philippines

Malaysia

Middle
Layer

passion-flower
butterfly

Indonesia

New
Guinea

INDIAN
OCEAN

Siproeta
stelenes
butterfly

Shrub Layer

kinkajou

AUSTRALIA

Herb
Layer

of the World

violet-tailed
sylph

ANTARCTICA

Hamadryas
arinome

chestnut-
capped

blue
morpho

red-legged
creeper

Papilio
androgeus
butterfly

puffbird

parakeet

butterfly

ocelot

butterfly

red-
honey